ALFRED's
CRED PERFORMER
COLLECTIONS

MW01152131

What Can I Pl...
Book 1: January & February Services

Arranged by Cindy Berry

10 Easily Prepared Piano Arrangements for January & February Services

Have you ever thought, "I wish I had *one* piano book that included appropriate hymn arrangements for the next couple of months"? As a church accompanist, I have shared that thought with you! *What Can I Play on Sunday?* is a series of six books, each book containing easily prepared pieces that are appropriate for a two-month period of the year. Book 1 is for January and February, Book 2 for March and April, and so on. Each book serves as a wonderful resource for your worship-planning needs for each season of the year. If your church uses Lectionary-based worship, these arrangements should be appropriate for those needs as well.

Book 1 contains arrangements that are especially appropriate for the months of January and February, and includes selections for Epiphany, Creation, Jesus' Baptism, Transfiguration, Ash Wednesday, Communion and Lent, as well as several general hymns. The other books in this series are as follows:

Book 2: March and April
Book 3: May and June
Book 4: July and August
Book 5: September and October
Book 6: November and December

I pray that you will find this series useful as you play your praises to God on Sundays, or use these arrangements for your own personal worship times.

Cindy Berry

Alfred

LET ALL THINGS NOW LIVING

Traditional Welsh Melody
("Ash Grove")
Arr. Cindy Berry

7

THIS IS MY FATHER'S WORLD

Franklin L. Sheppard
Arr. by Cindy Berry

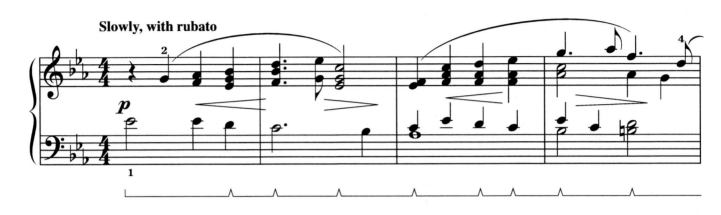

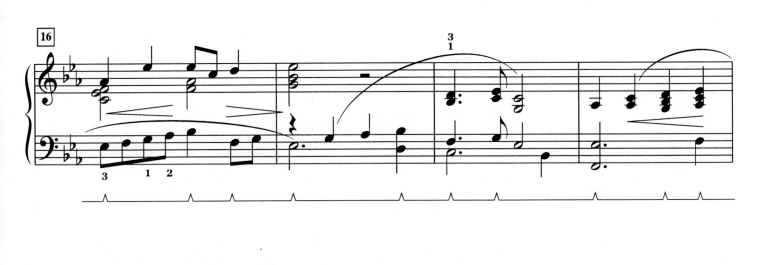

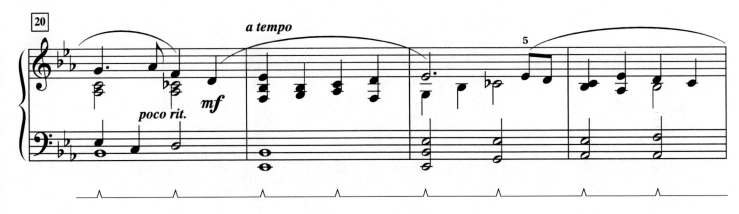

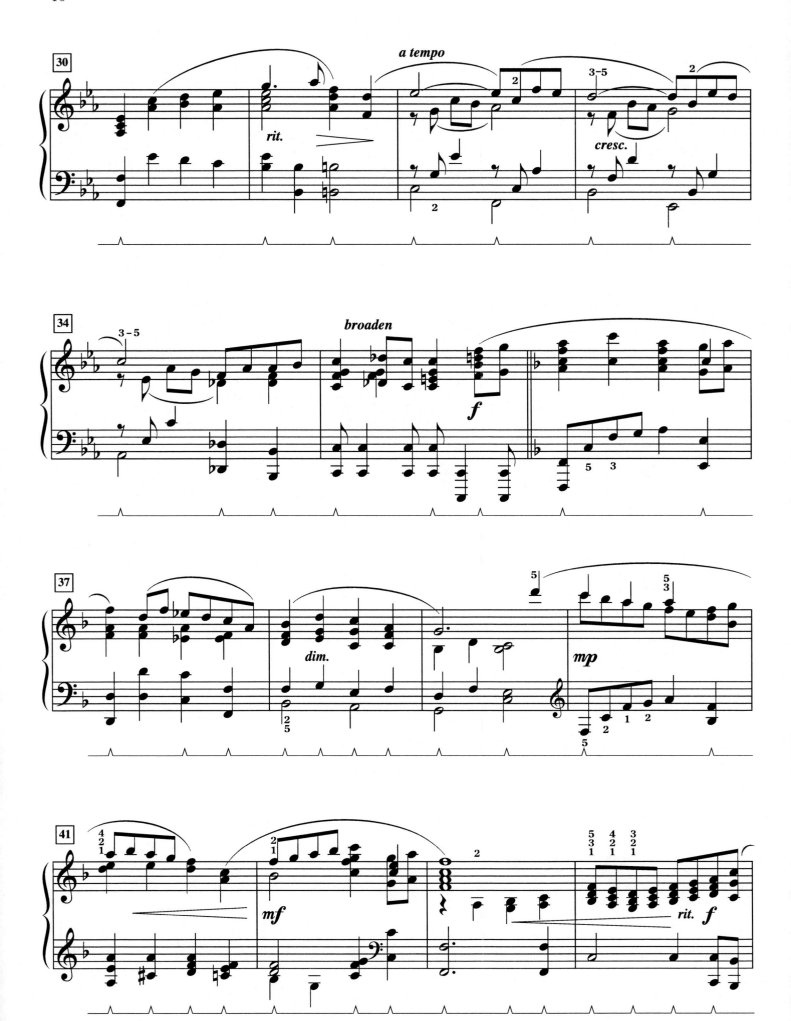

JESUS SHALL REIGN

John Hatton
Arr. by Cindy Berry

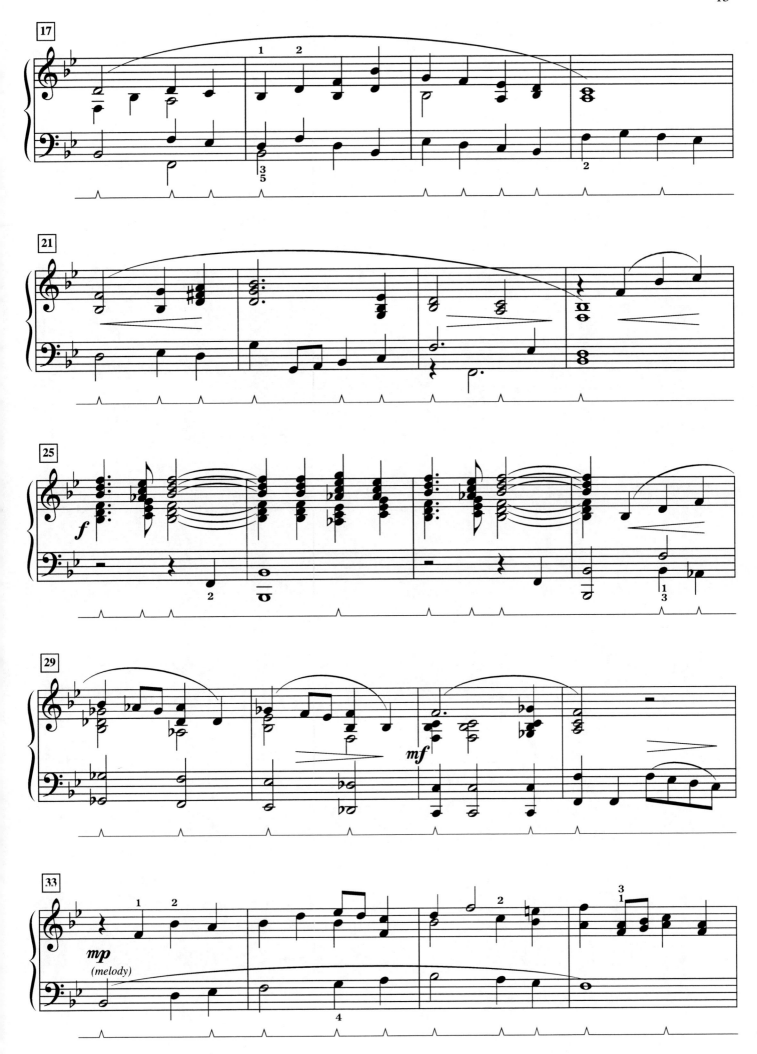

COME, HOLY SPIRIT, DOVE DIVINE

H. Percy Smith
Arr. by Cindy Berry

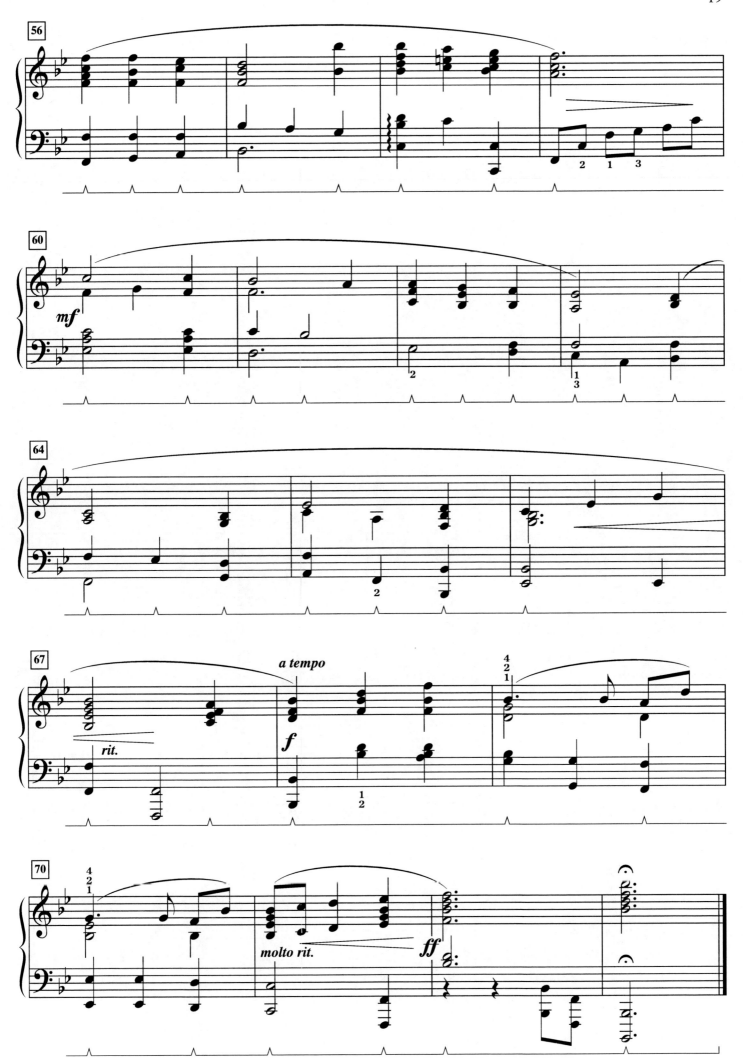

O ZION, HASTE

James Walch
Arr. by Cindy Berry

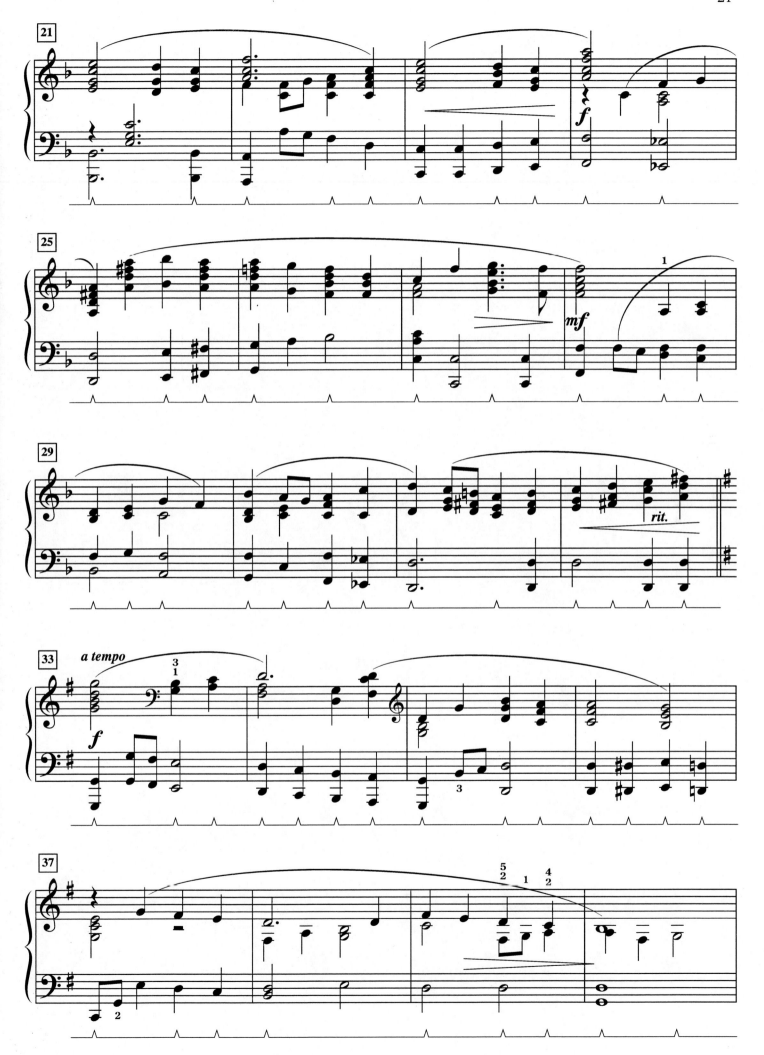

CHRIST, WHOSE GLORY FILLS THE SKIES

Johann G. Werner
Arr. by Cindy Berry

LORD, I WANT TO BE A CHRISTIAN

American Folk Hymn
Arr. by Cindy Berry

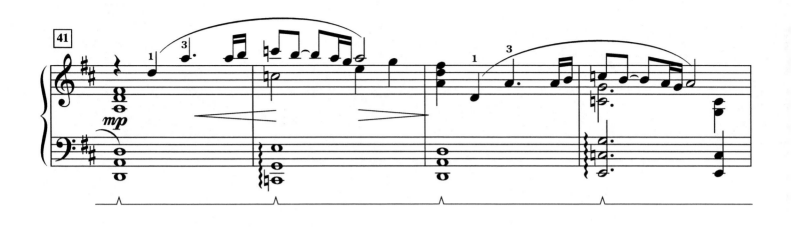

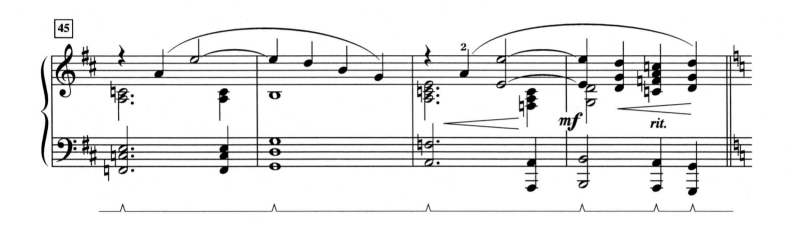

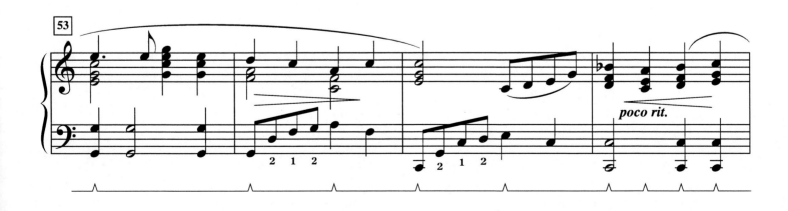

DEPTH OF MERCY WITH
SEARCH ME, O GOD

Carl M. von Weber
Edward J. Hopkins
Arr. by Cindy Berry

O God, Our Help in Ages Past

William Croft
Arr. by Cindy Berry

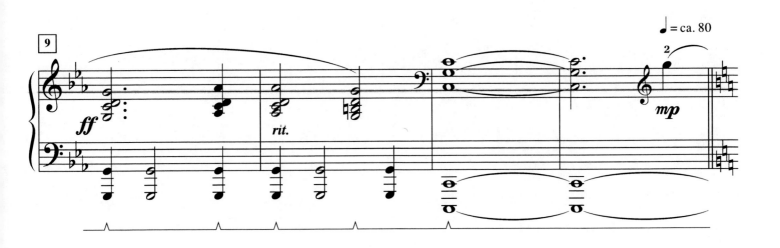

JESUS, KEEP ME NEAR THE CROSS WITH
IN THE CROSS OF CHRIST I GLORY

William Howard Doane
Ithamar D. Conkey
Arr. by Cindy Berry

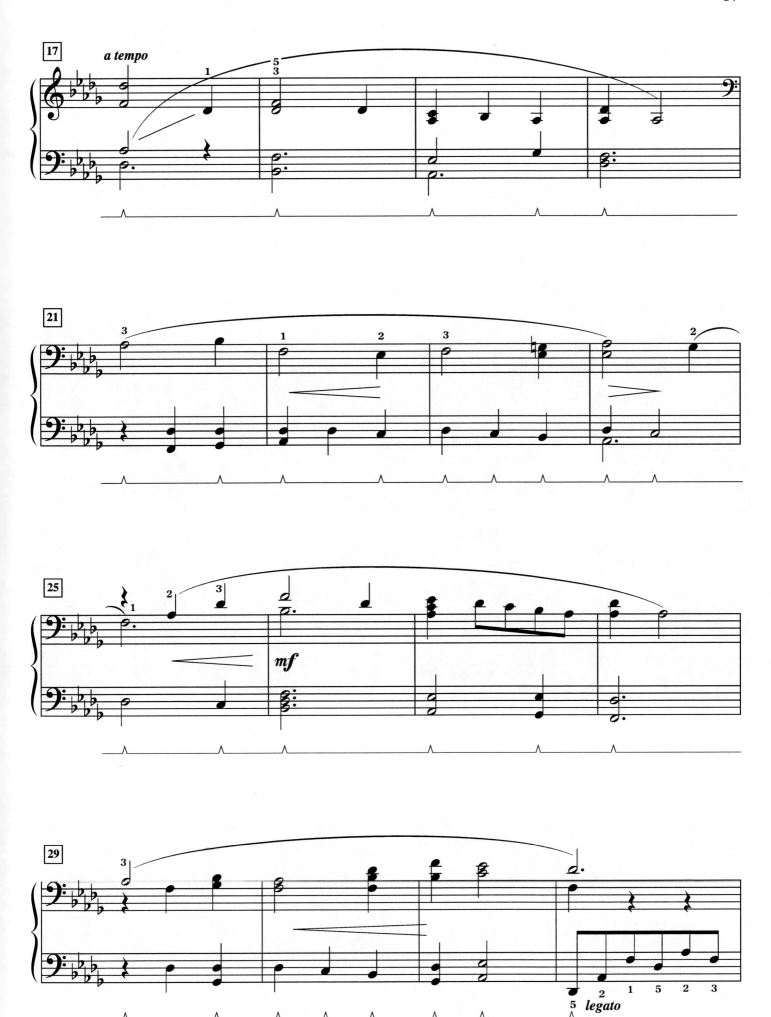